MW00564232

Lerner SPORTS

GREATEST OF ALL TIME TEAMS

G.O.A.T.
SOCCER TEAMS

MATT DOEDEN

Lerner Publications ◆ Minneapolis

Lerner Publications Company
An imprint of Lerner Publishing Group, Inc.
241 First Avenue North
Minneapolis, MN 55401 USA

For reading levels and more information, look up this title at www.lernerbooks.com.

Main body text set in Aptifer Sans LT Pro.Typeface provided by Linotype AG.

Designer: Kim Morales

Library of Congress Cataloging-in-Publication Data

Names: Doeden, Matt, author.
Title: G.O.A.T. soccer teams / Matt Doeden.
Description: Minneapolis : Lerner Publications, [2021] | Series: Greatest of all time teams (Lerner sports) | Includes bibliographical references and index. | Audience: Ages 7–11 | Audience: Grades 2–3 | Summary: "Soccer's best teams had superstar players, incredible goals, and epic victories. From Brazil's national team that featured the legendary Pelé to the 2019 US Women's National Team, meet the greatest soccer teams of all time"— Provided by publisher.
Identifiers: LCCN 2020009625 (print) | LCCN 2020009626 (ebook) | ISBN 9781728404424 (library binding) | ISBN 9781728418261 (ebook)
Subjects: LCSH: Soccer teams—Juvenile literature. | Soccer—Juvenile literature.
Classification: LCC GV943.25 .D62 2021 (print) | LCC GV943.25 (ebook) | DDC 796.334—dc23

LC record available at https://lccn.loc.gov/2020009625
LC ebook record available at https://lccn.loc.gov/2020009626

Manufactured in the United States of America
1-48500-49014-8/19/2020

TABLE OF CONTENTS

Lionel Messi has scored more than 600 career goals for Barcelona.

GOAL!

Soccer is the world's most popular sport. Superstars such as Pelé, Lionel Messi, and Marta thrill fans with their amazing moves, pinpoint passes, and blazing shots. But teams win and lose based on how well they work together. They need teamwork, great leaders, and perhaps a little luck.

FACTS AT A GLANCE

>> In the 2007 Women's World Cup, Germany didn't allow a single goal in six matches.

>> From 1958 to 1970, the Brazil men's national team won three out of four World Cups.

>> In 1999, Manchester United became the first English team to complete the treble. They won the Premier League, the FA Cup, and the Champions League.

>> In the 2008–2009 season, Barcelona competed for six trophies and won them all.

>> In 2019, the US Women's National Team (USWNT) outscored their opponents 24–3 on their way to winning the Women's World Cup.

In Europe, players make millions playing for the top pro teams in the world. Countries have their own leagues, such as the Premier League in Britain and La Liga in Spain. The biggest prize in Europe is the Champions League.

Fans love their favorite pro teams. But nothing excites most fans more than rooting for a team that represents their country. National teams with star-studded rosters compete in international tournaments such as the World Cup and Women's World Cup. The winners get bragging rights as the best in the world.

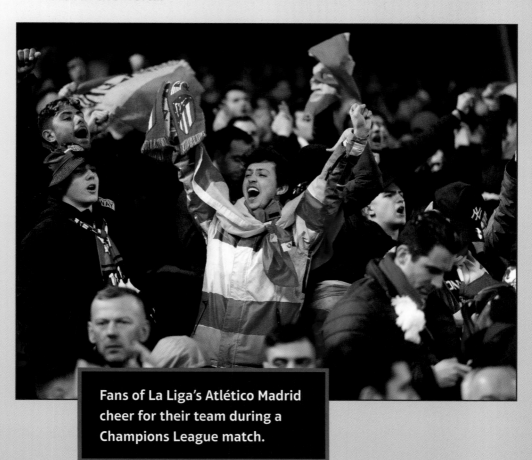

Fans of La Liga's Atlético Madrid cheer for their team during a Champions League match.

Team USA's Abby Wambach (*right*) controls the ball during a match against China. Wambach helped the United States win Olympic gold medals in 2004 and 2012 and the Women's World Cup in 2015.

But what makes a team great? Is it championships and trophies? Or record-setting performances? How do teams from different times and leagues compare to one another? Which team is the greatest of all time (G.O.A.T.), and how do fans decide?

As you learn more about the greatest teams of all time, think about how to compare them. Then decide the G.O.A.T. teams for yourself.

Birgit Prinz scored 14 career goals in Women's World Cup matches.

10 2007 GERMANY WOMEN'S NATIONAL TEAM

During the 2000s, Germany ruled women's soccer. The national team was built on pure scoring power. After winning the Women's World Cup in 2003, Germany was on a quest to win back-to-back titles.

They wasted no time reminding the world why they were the defending champs. Germany destroyed Argentina

Germany's Simone Laudehr makes a powerful play in the 2007 FIFA Women's World Cup final.

11–0 in the opening match—the start of one of the greatest performances in soccer history. Goalkeeper Nadine Angerer didn't allow a single goal in the team's six matches.

No one could keep up with Germany's balance of offense and defense in the knockout round. Germany beat North Korea and Norway to advance to the World Cup final against Brazil. German striker Birgit Prinz scored the match's first goal in the 52nd minute. Simone Laudehr added a second goal to give Germany the championship.

2007 GERMANY WOMEN'S NATIONAL TEAM STATS

▸▸▸ Germany outscored their opponents 21–0 in six matches.

▸▸▸ They scored 11 goals in their opening match against Argentina.

▸▸▸ Goalkeeper Nadine Angerer was named the tournament's best goalkeeper.

▸▸▸ Birgit Prinz led the team with five World Cup goals.

▸▸▸ They became the first team to win back-to-back Women's World Cups.

Zinedine Zidane runs with the ball past a Brazil defender.

9

1998 FRANCE MEN'S NATIONAL TEAM

Some teams are built on flashy scoring and exciting plays. Not France's 1998 men's national team. The French team was anything but flashy. Led by Thierry Henry and Zinedine Zidane, France won by mastering the basics of soccer. They played as a team, and they didn't make mistakes.

Thierry Henry played in four World Cups.

France hosted the 1998 World Cup, so the pressure was on for the team. The French fans badly wanted a winner. Their team delivered. France controlled the group round, winning all three matches by a combined score of 9–1. They thrilled fans in the knockout round with close victories over Paraguay, Italy, and Croatia. In the final, they faced a powerful Brazil team. Zidane was the hero, scoring two goals in a 3–0 victory. The party was on all around the country as France secured its place as one of the greatest soccer teams in history.

1998 FRANCE MEN'S NATIONAL TEAM STATS

>>> France won their first World Cup title.

>>> Thierry Henry led the team with three goals.

>>> Fabien Barthez was named the World Cup's best goalkeeper, allowing only two goals in seven matches.

>>> France outscored its World Cup opponents 15–2.

>>> France trailed for only one minute during the entire World Cup tournament.

Real Madrid players lined up for this photo before the 1957 European Cup final against ACF Fiorentina.

NO. 8
1956-1957
REAL
MADRID

Few soccer clubs have a longer winning tradition than Spain's Real Madrid has. Their 1956–1957 squad may have been their finest. The team signed top talent from all around the globe. In the modern game, that's common. But in the late 1950s, it was a new way to win.

No player was more important than Alfredo Di Stéfano. The powerful, quick striker from Argentina was a threat to

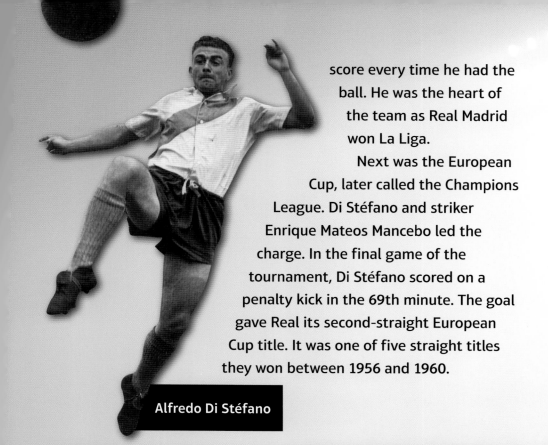

score every time he had the ball. He was the heart of the team as Real Madrid won La Liga.

Next was the European Cup, later called the Champions League. Di Stéfano and striker Enrique Mateos Mancebo led the charge. In the final game of the tournament, Di Stéfano scored on a penalty kick in the 69th minute. The goal gave Real its second-straight European Cup title. It was one of five straight titles they won between 1956 and 1960.

Alfredo Di Stéfano

1956–1957 REAL MADRID STATS

- ▶▶▶ Real Madrid won La Liga with a 20–6–4 record.
- ▶▶▶ They outscored their La Liga opponents 74–35.
- ▶▶▶ Alfredo Di Stéfano led La Liga with 31 goals.
- ▶▶▶ Enrique Mateos Mancebo was second on the team with 14 goals.
- ▶▶▶ Alfredo Di Stéfano scored seven goals in eight European Cup matches.

1998-1999
MANCHESTER
UNITED

NO.

By the end of the 1990s, the Manchester United Red
Devils were the power of England's Premier League. They
were stronger than ever in 1998–1999. Stars such as David
Beckham, Andy Cole, and Dwight Yorke led the team. They
won the Premier League with a 22–3–13 record.

The wins kept coming in the FA Cup, a tournament
featuring teams from around England. Manchester United

Manchester United's David Beckham on the field at the final match of the UEFA Champions League

beat Newcastle in the final. It was the second trophy of the season for the Red Devils.

Only the Champions League remained. The Red Devils had the chance to complete the rare treble by winning the Premier League, the FA Cup, and the Champions League in the same season. And that's what they did. After going 2–0–4 in the group round, the Red Devils caught fire in the knockout round. They capped it off with a thrilling 2–1 comeback victory over Bayern Munich in the final.

1998–1999 MANCHESTER UNITED STATS

>>> The Red Devils were the first English team to win the treble.

>>> They scored eight goals in a single match against Nottingham Forest.

>>> They outscored their Premier League opponents 83–37.

>>> Dwight Yorke led the team in goals with 29.

>>> Manchester United scored two goals in the last three minutes of the Champions League final to win 2–1.

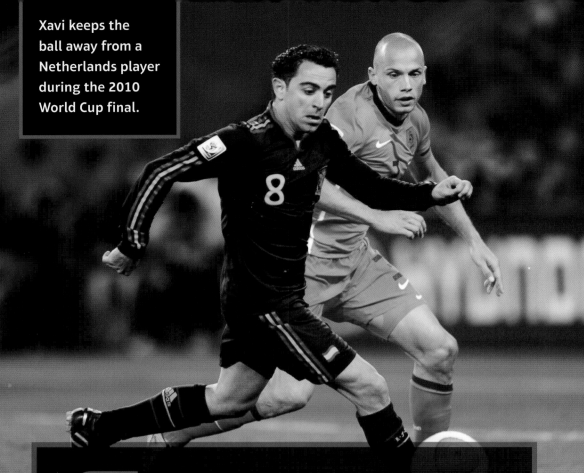

Xavi keeps the ball away from a Netherlands player during the 2010 World Cup final.

NO. 6
2010 SPAIN MEN'S NATIONAL TEAM

Most great teams are known for scoring amazing goals. Not the 2010 Spain national team. Spain was built on great goalkeeping and punishing defense. Their roster was loaded with some of the biggest stars in soccer, including Xavi, David Villa, and Sergio Ramos. Spain could score, but they really shined at defending their goal. At times, it seemed almost impossible to get the ball past goalkeeper Iker Casillas.

Spain's quest for the nation's first World Cup title didn't begin well. They lost their opening match 1–0 to Switzerland. But they bounced back. Spain won the rest of their games in group play to advance to the knockout round. Then Spain went on an amazing run. The team didn't allow a single goal in four matches. They defeated the Netherlands 1–0 in the final to win the World Cup and lay their claim as the greatest defensive team of all time.

Iker Casillas

2010 SPAIN MEN'S NATIONAL TEAM STATS

>>> Spain won all four of their World Cup knockout round matches by the same score, 1–0.

>>> They became Spain's first national team to win the World Cup.

>>> David Villa led the team in the World Cup with five goals.

>>> Iker Casillas won the Golden Glove award as the World Cup's best goalkeeper.

>>> Spain won the World Cup despite scoring just eight goals in seven matches.

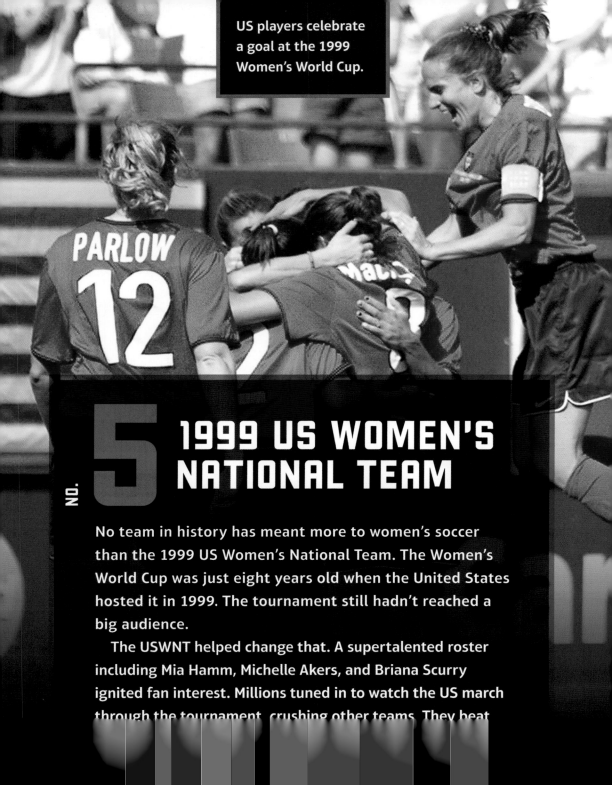

US players celebrate a goal at the 1999 Women's World Cup.

5

1999 US WOMEN'S NATIONAL TEAM

No team in history has meant more to women's soccer than the 1999 US Women's National Team. The Women's World Cup was just eight years old when the United States hosted it in 1999. The tournament still hadn't reached a big audience.

The USWNT helped change that. A supertalented roster including Mia Hamm, Michelle Akers, and Briana Scurry ignited fan interest. Millions tuned in to watch the US march through the tournament, crushing other teams. They beat

Germany and Brazil in the knockout round to set up the final with China.

The scoreless game went to penalty kicks. Brandi Chastain booted the game-winner, thrilling fans in the stadium and millions more watching on TV. The popularity of women's soccer has only grown since 1999. Many credit the USWNT and their exciting run for fueling that growth.

Mia Hamm

1999 USWNT STATS

>>> The USWNT won all six of their Women's World Cup matches.

>>> They outscored Women's World Cup opponents 18–3.

>>> The USWNT became the first team to win the Women's World Cup twice.

>>> More than 90,000 fans packed the Rose Bowl to watch the final. That set a record for the most people at a women's sporting event.

>>> In the tournament, 10 different US players scored goals.

Pelé (*center*) raises his arms after a teammate's goal during the 1970 World Cup final. Pelé played in four World Cups for Brazil.

4 1970 BRAZIL MEN'S NATIONAL TEAM

Brazil won its first World Cup in 1958, starting a dynasty that lasted 12 years. The team won three World Cups over that time. Brazil had the world's greatest player, Pelé. The team delivered a fierce attacking style that few others could match. They were not a great defensive team, but they didn't need great defense to win. They were so good at scoring goals that their defense almost didn't matter.

Fans loved Pelé's dazzling moves with the ball.

The greatest team of Brazil's dynasty was the 1970 squad. They failed to make the knockout round in the 1966 World Cup. So Brazil came out with something to prove in 1970. The team won all three of their matches in group play. Then Pelé and his teammates steamrolled everyone in the knockout round. They finished their championship run with a 4–1 thumping of Italy in the final. Brazil proved they were still the world's greatest team.

1970 BRAZIL MEN'S NATIONAL TEAM STATS

>>> Brazil outscored their opponents 19–7 in six World Cup matches.

>>> They won their third World Cup in 12 years.

>>> Jairzinho led the team with seven goals.

>>> Pelé was second on the team with four goals.

>>> More than 107,000 fans packed the stadium in Mexico City, Mexico, to watch Brazil beat Italy.

AFC Ajax players and coaches pose with the European Cup in 1973.

NO. 3

1972-1973 AFC AJAX

In the early 1970s, the Dutch team AFC Ajax was the greatest in the world. They didn't just win trophies. They changed the way the game was played. Ajax manager Rinus Michels created a new style of play called Total Football. Under Michels's system, Ajax players didn't fill full-time roles. Instead, they moved from position

Johan Cruyff scored three goals for the Netherlands in the 1974 World Cup.

to position as the game changed. Any player could fill any role.

It was a whole new way to play soccer. Other teams didn't know how to stop it. Ajax and star striker Johan Cruyff ruled the Dutch league, going 30–4–0. In the European Cup, they outscored opponents 15–4 on their way to claiming the title. It was the peak of one of the greatest dynasties in club soccer history. Ajax left a lasting impact on how the game is played.

1972-1973 AJAX STATS

>>> Ajax outscored their opponents 102–18.

>>> They won their 16th league championship.

>>> The team won its third straight European Cup.

>>> Johan Cruyff led the team with 26 goals.

>>> Ajax outscored their European Cup opponents 15–4.

NO. 2

2008-2009 BARCELONA

Barcelona has been a superpower in La Liga for decades.
Their greatest season, however, came in a year when
some thought they might struggle. The team had a new
manager, Pep Guardiola. Two of their biggest stars, Deco
and Ronaldinho, had moved to other clubs.

Yet the big changes didn't slow down Barcelona. Their
tough, gritty style helped them win La Liga. Samuel
Eto'o, Lionel Messi, and Thierry Henry supplied the
goal-scoring punch.

Samuel Eto'o led Barcelona's scoring attack with 34 goals.

Winning La Liga was just the start. Barcelona crushed Athletic Bilbao 4–1 to claim Spain's national title. Then they beat Manchester United 2–0 to win the Champions League and the treble. Barcelona also won the Spanish Super Cup, UEFA Super Cup, and the Club World Cup tournaments. No other team has ever won all six tournaments in a single season.

2008-2009 BARCELONA STATS

>>> Barcelona went 27–6–5 in La Liga.

>>> They outscored La Liga opponents 105–35.

>>> Barcelona won six major trophies.

>>> Lionel Messi scored 32 goals and was named FIFA World Player of the Year.

>>> They outscored opponents 14–5 in the knockout round of the Champions League.

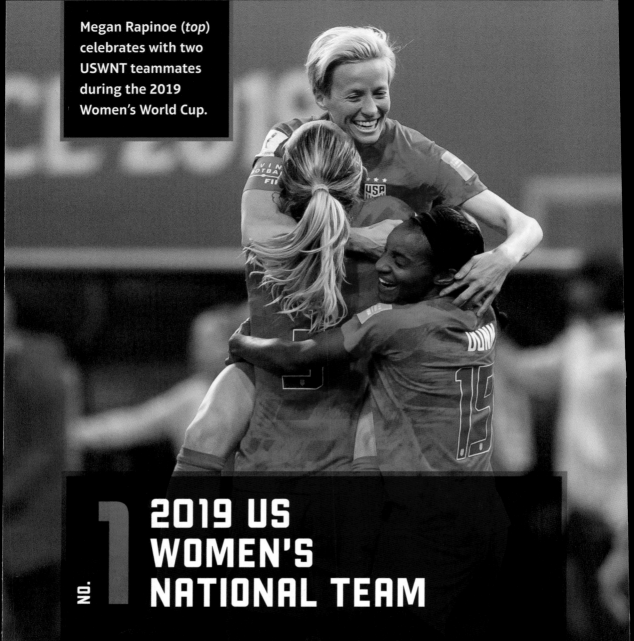

Megan Rapinoe (*top*) celebrates with two USWNT teammates during the 2019 Women's World Cup.

NO. 1 — 2019 US WOMEN'S NATIONAL TEAM

The 2019 USWNT was the greatest force in soccer history. The team was led by goal-scorers Carli Lloyd, Megan Rapinoe, and Alex Morgan. They lost just one game all season in a friendly match against France.

In June, the USWNT took the Women's World Cup by storm. In their first match, they beat Thailand by a stunning

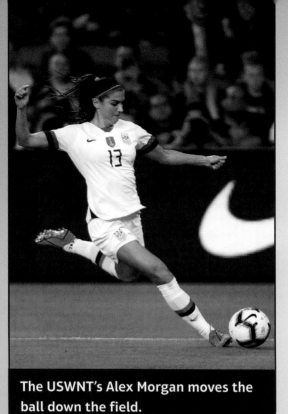

The USWNT's Alex Morgan moves the ball down the field.

score of 13–0. That offensive outburst set the tone. The powerful US team marched through the tournament, outscoring their opponents 26–3. Their quick-strike offense and lockdown defense left other teams helpless. A 2–0 victory over the Netherlands in the final capped off their amazing run. It gave the USWNT their second Women's World Cup title in a row. *Time* magazine named the members of the squad its 2019 Athletes of the Year.

2019 USWNT STATS

>>> The USWNT had a 20–1–3 record.

>>> They outscored their opponents 77–16.

>>> Carli Lloyd led the team in goals with 16.

>>> Goalkeeper Alyssa Naeher averaged less than one goal allowed per game.

>>> The USWNT outscored their Women's World Cup opponents 26–3.

YOUR
G.O.A.T.

ASK 10 FANS TO MAKE THEIR OWN LIST OF
SOCCER'S GREATEST TEAMS AND YOU'LL
PROBABLY GET 10 DIFFERENT LISTS. That's because
there's no right or wrong way to rank teams from different
eras and leagues. As you read about some of the great
teams on this list, you may have formed your own opinions
about them. What do you value most? Is it trophies and
championships? Does winning close, nail-biting matches
mean as much as winning blowouts?

If you disagree with this list, make your own! Check out
books and websites on soccer's greatest teams and players.
Talk to fellow soccer fans about who they consider the
greatest. Come up with your own top 10, and crown your
greatest of all time. Then have a friend do the same and
compare your results. Where do you agree? Where do you
disagree?

SOCCER FACTS

>>> Brazil has won five World Cups, more than any other nation. The United States leads the way with four Women's World Cups.

>>> From 1956 to 1977, Pelé scored a record 1,281 goals. His record includes goals in international play as well as in pro matches.

>>> In the 2007 World Cup qualifying round, Belgium's Christian Benteke scored a goal just 8.1 seconds into a match.

>>> In 2015, England was knocked out of the Women's World Cup when Laura Bassett accidentally scored on her own goal.

>>> The first World Cup was held in 1930. Uruguay defeated Argentina 4–2 to claim the championship.

GLOSSARY

Champions League: a tournament of pro teams to decide the best team in Europe

dynasty: a long period of dominance by a team, usually including multiple championships

final: a tournament's championship game

friendly: a match that is not part of a league or tournament

group round: the stage of a tournament in which teams in a group play one another. The top two teams advance to the knockout round.

knockout round: the stage of a tournament in which a game's winning team advances to the next round and the losing team is out of the tournament

penalty kick: a free kick at the goal allowed for certain fouls or to determine the winner of some games

pro: a person who plays a sport for money

striker: a player whose main job is to score goals

treble: a feat achieved by holding three major trophies, including a league title, a national title, and the Champions League title in the same year

LEARN MORE

FIFA World Cup
https://www.fifa.com/worldcup/

Fishman, Jon M. *Soccer's G.O.A.T.: Pele, Lionel Messi, and More.* Minneapolis: Lerner Publications, 2020.

Scheff, Matt. *The World Cup: Soccer's Greatest Tournament.* Minneapolis: Lerner Publications, 2021.

Sports Illustrated Kids: Soccer
https://www.sikids.com/tag/soccer

U.S. Soccer
https://www.ussoccer.com/

Weakland, Mark. *Soccer Records.* Mankato, MN: Black Rabbit Books, 2021.

INDEX

PHOTO ACKNOWLEDGMENTS

Image credits: Jean Catuffe/Getty Images, p. 1; Tim Clayton - Corbis/Getty Images, p. 4; Michael Regan - UEFA/Getty Images, p. 6; Christian Petersen/Getty Images, p. 7; Carmen Jaspersen/picture-alliance/dpa/AP Images, p. 8; Cao zichen - Imaginechina via AP Images, p. 9; Simon Wilkinson/EMPICS/Getty Images, p. 10; Matthew Ashton - EMPICS/Getty Images, p. 11; Real Madrid/Getty Images, p. 12; Amarhgil/Wikimedia Commons (public domain), p. 13; Neal Simpson - EMPICS/Getty Images, p. 14; Alain Gadoffre/Icon Sport/Getty Images, p. 15; PIERRE-PHILIPPE MARCOU/AFP/Getty Images, p. 16; Steve Haag/Getty Images, p. 17; TIMOTHY A. CLARY/AFP/Getty Images, p. 18; Jed Jacobsohn/Getty Images, p. 19; Heidtmann/picture alliance/Getty Images, p. 20; AP Photo, p. 21; Central Press/Hulton Archive/Getty Images, p. 22; Heinz Wieseler/picture alliance/Getty Images, p. 23; Christian Liewig - Corbis/Getty Images, p. 24; Philippe Perusseau/Icon Sport/Getty Images, p. 25; TF-Images/Getty Images, p. 26; Meg Oliphant/Getty Images, p. 27; Todd Strand/Independent Picture Service, p. 28 (ball). Design elements: EFKS/Shutterstock.com; RaiDztor/Shutterstock.com; MIKHAIL GRACHIKOV/Shutterstock.com; Vitalii Kozyrskyi/Shutterstock.com; ESB Professional/Shutterstock.com; MEandMO/Shutterstock.com; Roman Sotola/Shutterstock.com.

Cover: Jean Catuffe/Getty Images. Design elements: EFKS/Shutterstock.com; RaiDztor/Shutterstock.com; MIKHAIL GRACHIKOV/Shutterstock.com; ijaydesign99/Shutterstock.com.